little Miss Busy

by Roger Hargreaves

Little Miss Busy loved nothing more than to be hard at work, keeping herself busy.

As busy as a bee.

In fact, as busy as a hive of bees.

Every day she would get up at three o'clock in the morning.

Then, Little Miss Busy,
would read a chapter from her favourite book.

It was called:
"Work is Good for You".

And then she would get down to the housework.

She would begin by tidying up,
and then sweeping,
and dusting,
and scrubbing,
and polishing,
until everything was spotless.

She would clean her house from top to bottom
and then from bottom to top, just to make sure.

She even dusted the bread and polished the butter.

She wasn't happy unless she was busy working.

And she didn't rest all day long, not for a minute,
not even for a second.

From three o'clock in the morning
until after midnight.

That was until last Monday.

Little Miss Busy wasn't up at three o'clock.

She wasn't up by six o'clock.

She wasn't even out of bed by nine o'clock.

She was ill.

"Oh, calamity!" she cried.

"I won't be able to do any work!"

She telephoned Doctor Make-you-well.

Five minutes later he was at her bedside.

He asked her to put out her tongue.

He examined her throat.

And he looked at her hands and feet.

“What you need is rest, a lot of rest,”
he said, with a broad smile.

"A lot of rest," repeated Little Miss Busy to herself.

"Oh, calamity!"

There was a loud THUMP!

Which was the sound of Little Miss Busy
falling over backwards,
on to the bed,
luckily for her.

On Tuesday, Mr Strong
called to see Little Miss Busy.

He brought her 72 eggs.

Go on, count them.

"There is nothing like eggs
for giving you strength," said Mr Strong.

By the seventy-second egg,
Little Miss Busy was feeling much better.

That was, until Mr Strong said,
"Now you must rest to get your strength up."

There was a loud THUMP!

Which was the sound of Little Miss Busy
falling over backwards,
on to the bed,
luckily for her.

On Wednesday, Mr Greedy
came to visit.

He brought an enormous bowl of food.

"I always find that eating a big meal
makes me feel better," said Mr Greedy.

Little Miss Busy ate the lot.

She felt better than ever.

That was until Mr Greedy said,
"Now you must rest to let your stomach settle."

There was a loud THUMP!

And you know what that was, don't you?

That's right!

Little Miss Busy had fallen over backwards.

On Thursday, Mr Nonsense
popped in to see Little Miss Busy.

He brought her … an umbrella!

"Hello," he said.
"I hear you're feeling well. You don't need a rest … "

Little Miss Busy jumped for joy, right out of bed.
" … you need a holiday!" finished Mr Nonsense.

There was a loud THUMP!
That's right.
"There, you look better already," said Mr Nonsense,
and left …

… by the open window.

Little Miss Busy picked herself up.

A small smile formed on her face.

Something Mr Nonsense had said
had actually made sense.

She had never thought of going on holiday before.

The more she thought about it the happier she felt.

She thought of all the fun things she could do.

There was the planning and organising,
there was all the shopping she would have to do,
there was the packing,
and she would have to learn the language,
and read lots of books about the place she was going to.

What a lot of work!

Little Miss Busy smiled happily.

The following Thursday, she was awake
at three o'clock in the morning.

Everything was ready.

Little Miss Busy had had one of the
busiest weeks of her life.

Which is saying something!

She had only one thing left to do.

And that was ...

… to learn how to twiddle her thumbs!

•RETURN THIS WHOLE PAGE•

3 Great Offers For Mr Men Fans

1 FREE Door Hangers and Posters

In every Mr Men and Little Miss Book like this one you will find a special token. Collect 6 and we will send you either a brilliant Mr. Men or Little Miss poster and a Mr Men or Little Miss double sided, full colour, bedroom door hanger. Apply using the coupon overleaf, enclosing six tokens and a 50p coin for your choice of two items.

Egmont World tokens can be used towards any other Egmont World / World International token scheme promotions., in early learning and story / activity books.

Posters: Tick your preferred choice of either Mr Men ☐ or Little Miss ☐

Door Hangers: Choose from: Mr. Nosey & Mr Muddle ☐, Mr Greedy & Mr Lazy ☐, Mr Tickle & Mr Grumpy ☐, Mr Slow & Mr Busy ☐, Mr Messy & Mr Quiet ☐, Mr Perfect & Mr Forgetful ☐, Little Miss Fun & Little Miss Late ☐, Little MIss Helpful & Little Miss Tidy ☐, Little Miss Busy & Little Miss Brainy ☐, Little Miss Star & Little Miss Fun ☐. (Please tick)

2 Mr Men Library Boxes

Keep your growing collection of Mr Men and Little Miss books in these superb library boxes. With an integral carrying handle and stay-closed fastener, these full colour, plastic boxes are fantastic. They are just £5.49 each including postage. Order overleaf.

3 Join The Club

To join the fantastic Mr Men & Little Miss Club, check out the page overleaf NOW!

Allow 28 days for delivery. We reserve the right to change the terms of this offer at any time but we offer a 14 day money back guarantee. The money-back guarantee does not affect your statutory rights. Birthday and Christmas cards are sent care of parent/guardians in advance of the day. After 31/12/00 please call to check that the offer details are still correct.

•RETURN THIS WHOLE PAGE•

When you become a member of the fantastic Mr Men and Little Miss Club you'll receive a personal letter from Mr Happy and Little Miss Giggles, a club badge with your name, and a superb Welcome Pack (pictured below right).

You'll also get birthday and Christmas cards from the Mr Men and Little Misses, 2 newsletters crammed with special offers, privileges and news, and a copy of the 12 page Mr Men catalogue which includes great party ideas.

If it were on sale in the shops, the Welcome Pack alone might cost around £13. But a year's membership is just £9.99 (plus 73p postage) with a 14 day money-back guarantee if you are not delighted!

HOW TO APPLY To apply for any of these three great offers, ask an adult to complete the coupon below and send it with appropriate payment and tokens (where required) to: Mr Men Offers, PO Box 7, Manchester M19 2HD. Credit card orders for Club membership ONLY by telephone, please call: 01403 242727.

To be completed by an adult

❑ **1.** Please send a poster and door hanger as selected overleaf. I enclose six tokens and a 50p coin for post (coin not required if you are also taking up 2. or 3. below).

❑ **2.** Please send __ Mr Men Library case(s) and __ Little Miss Library case(s) at £5.49 each.

❑ **3.** Please enrol the following in the Mr Men & Little Miss Club at £10.72 (inc postage)

Fan's Name:________________ Fan's Address:________________

____

________________ Post Code:________________ Date of birth:___/___/___

Your Name:________________ Your Address:________________

____

Post Code:__________ Name of parent or guardian (if not you):________________

Total amount due: £________ (£5.49 per Library Case, £10.72 per Club membership)

❑ I enclose a cheque or postal order payable to Egmont World Limited.

❑ Please charge my MasterCard / Visa account.

Card number: | | | | | | | | | | | | | | | |

Expiry Date: ____/____ Signature: ________________

Data Protection Act: If you do **not** wish to receive other family offers from us or companies we recommend, please tick this box ❑. Offer applies to UK only